To Arden from Grandma K.
Grandpa K. May 1998

MY BROWN
BEAR BARNEY
IN TROUBLE

By Dorothy Butler
Illustrated by Elizabeth Fuller

Greenwillow Books
NEW YORK

For my granddaughter Bridget
—D. B.

For my husband, Hugh
—E. F.

Pen and ink and watercolor paints were used
for the full-color art.
The text type is Goudy Old Style.
Text copyright © 1993 by Dorothy Butler
Illustrations copyright © 1993 by Elizabeth Fuller
All rights reserved. No part of this book
may be reproduced or utilized in any form
or by any means, electronic or mechanical,
including photocopying, recording, or by
any information storage and retrieval
system, without permission in writing
from the Publisher, Greenwillow Books,
a division of William Morrow & Company, Inc.,
1350 Avenue of the Americas, New York, NY 10019.
Printed in Singapore by Tien Wah Press
First Edition   10 9 8 7 6 5 4 3 2 1

Library of Congress Cataloging-in-Publication Data
Butler, Dorothy (date)
My brown bear Barney in trouble / by Dorothy Butler ;
illustrated by Elizabeth Fuller.
p.   cm.
Summary: A little girl and her brown bear Barney have
a busy week, getting into all kinds of mischief.
ISBN 0-688-10521-1 (trade). ISBN 0-688-10522-X (lib.)
[1. Teddy bears—Fiction.]
I. Fuller, Elizabeth (Elizabeth A.), ill.
II. Title.   PZ7.B976Mz   1993
[E]—dc20   90-24776   CIP   AC

On Monday my brown bear Barney
and I played in our backyard.

We dug a deep hole.

We poured in lots of water.

We floated our boat on the water.

And we both fell in.
My mother was not very pleased.

On Tuesday my brown bear Barney and
our old dog Charlie and I played with my friend Fred.

We rode our bikes very fast around Fred's house.

We climbed our special tree and threw nuts at each other.

We painted our faces like clowns.

And we painted shoes and socks on Fred's baby sister.
Fred's mother was not very pleased.

On Wednesday my brown bear Barney and I
went shopping with my mother and my little brother.

We pushed my little brother in the cart.

We helped my mother choose the groceries.

We got buried in boxes of cornflakes.

And Barney fell into the freezer with the ice cream.
The supermarket man was not very pleased.

On Thursday my brown bear Barney and I went to
the dentist with my mother and my little brother.

We minded my little brother in the waiting room.

My brown bear Barney sat on an old man's lap
while I tidied up the books.

My little brother put on the old man's hat.

And then he emptied a lady's bag onto the floor.
The lady was not very pleased.
But the old man chuckled.

On Friday my mother took my brown bear Barney,
my friend Fred, and me to the library.

Barney got stuck in the automatic doors.

Then he escaped up an escalator, and we had to chase him.

My friend Fred and I helped a librarian push a heavy book cart.

Then we had a fight over our favorite book, and I won.
Some people looked rather angry.
But our special library lady smiled at us.

On Saturday my mother and my father and my little brother
and our old dog Charlie and I went to see my grandmother.

Barney and I dressed up in Granny's clothes.

We took Granny's cat for a walk.

We watered the flowers for Granny.

And then we cleaned her windows.
My mother and father were not very pleased.
But Granny didn't mind.

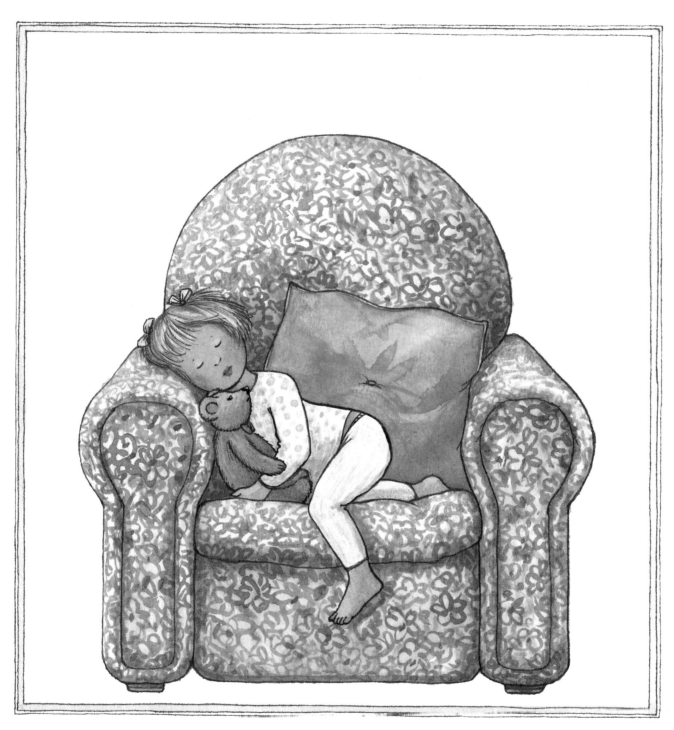

On Sunday my brown bear Barney and I
were very tired.

We read stories to each other.

We made a spaceship with our building blocks.

We tidied up our bedroom.

And in the afternoon we both took a nice nap.
My mother and father were very pleased.
But my brown bear Barney was bored.

"Never mind, Barney," I told him.
"It's Monday again tomorrow!"